WALTER THE LAZY MOUSE

Books by Marjorie Flack

WALTER THE LAZY MOUSE
ANGUS AND THE CAT
ANGUS AND THE DUCKS
ANGUS LOST
THE NEW PET
TIM TADPOLE AND THE GREAT BULLFROG
WAG-TAIL BESS

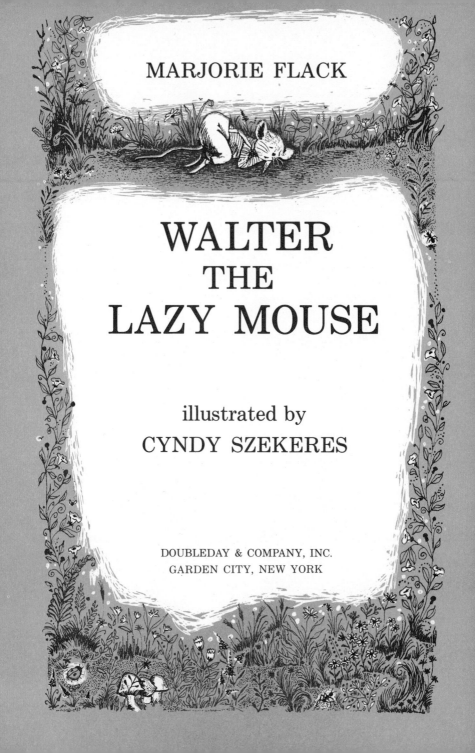

MARJORIE FLACK

WALTER
THE
LAZY MOUSE

illustrated by
CYNDY SZEKERES

DOUBLEDAY & COMPANY, INC.
GARDEN CITY, NEW YORK

ISBN: 0-385-01078-8

Library of Congress Catalog Card Number 62–16500
Illustrations Copyright © 1963 by Cynthia Szekeres Prozzo
Copyright 1937 by Marjorie Flack Larsson
All Rights Reserved
Printed in the United States of America

9   8   7   6   5   4

A Zephyr Book

WALTER THE LAZY MOUSE

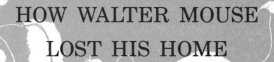

HOW WALTER MOUSE
LOST HIS HOME

Once upon a time there was a small young mouse named Walter. Walter lived in Mouse Village in a very nice house with his father and mother and five brothers and six sisters and they were a very busy mouse family—all but Walter. Walter was a lazy young mouse.

In the morning, Walter was never quite dressed by the time his sisters and his brothers were having their breakfast, and when they started off for school, Walter would still be eating his cereal.

Then he would run all the way to school, but no matter how fast he ran, somehow Walter would always be late.

When Miss Gray, his teacher, would ask Walter, "How much is two and two?" Walter would think and then he would count his fingers, but he was so slow that by the time he said "Five!" the teacher had forgotten the question and was busy with someone else.

When Walter went roller skating, he was so slow he could never catch up with his feet.

When Walter played football he was so slow he was always in the way of the other players.

At first, Walter's father and mother were greatly concerned because their little son was so lazy. They tried to hurry him and then they tried to punish him, but it did no good. Walter only seemed to grow lazier and slower. So since they were very busy mice with eleven other children to worry about, they gave it up.

As time went on, Walter became so slow he never even saw his father or mother or sisters or brothers, because on school days, by the time Walter was up in the morning, his father had gone to the office and his mother had gone shopping and his sisters and brothers had all gone to school. By the time Walter got to school they were all home for lunch,

and when Walter arrived home for lunch they had all left again. Walter was so slow that by the time he got home from school every night he was so late that the whole family had eaten their dinner and gone to bed. And on Saturdays and Sundays Walter never got out of bed at all.

So, after a few months of this, Walter's father and mother and sisters and brothers had not seen him for so long they forgot all about Walter. To be sure, his mother would sometimes say, "I wonder who left this empty bowl on the table," or "What became of that piece of pie I left in the pantry?" But she was a very busy mother and did not give it a second thought.

One spring evening when Walter came home from school, he went to the kitchen to find some food. When he opened the door he saw that the kitchen looked very strange. There was no stove, no table, no chairs. He went to the pantry and it was bare; not a crumb of food could he find. Walter went into the dining room; that too was empty. He went into

the living room; not a bit of furniture was in it. Walter ran up the stairs and into his room. His bed was gone, his chair was gone, everything was gone!

He looked in his closet and even his clothes were gone. Then Walter knew! He knew that his father and his mother and his sisters and his brothers had all moved away and that they had forgotten all about him!

Poor Walter did not know what to do. He was hungry and there was no food to eat and he was sleepy but there was no bed to sleep on. So Walter started out to find the family.

Down the street he ran, but he did not know where to go, so Walter just kept on running. On and on he ran until soon there were no more houses in sight and Walter felt very depressed.

Never before in his life had he been so far from home and by now he was so hungry he was no longer sleepy. The moon was high overhead, everything looked strange, but Walter did not know what to do so he kept on running. Soon he found himself in a thick forest and before he knew it Walter had lost the road.

Walter was tired. He was hungry. He did not know where his home was, he did not know where he was, so he sat down and he cried.

He cried and he cried, but it did him no good because there was no one to hear him, no one to feel sorry for him, no one to help him.

So Walter stopped crying and just sat there alone in the great forest. Soon he heard voices singing. So Walter scrambled through the forest; over stones, in the shadow of great mushrooms, on he went, trying to find the singers. Louder and louder grew the music and then Walter could hardly believe his eyes. He found himself at the edge of a great pond and all about him were creatures he had never seen the like of before.

They all had great bulging eyes. Some were small, so much smaller than Walter they made him feel large, and they sang in little high voices. Others were larger, a little larger than Walter, and they sang with medium-sized voices, but there was one huge creature, who was so huge he made Walter feel very small and he sang in a great deep voice like a bass drum.

Walter crept up to a tiny little creature and he whispered, "Have you seen my father and mother and sisters and brothers go by?" But the little creature did not hear him and went on singing. So Walter asked in a little louder voice, "Have you seen my father and mother and sisters and brothers go by?" But the little creature still did not hear

him because they all were making such a racket. Then Walter shouted as loud as he could shout, "HAVE YOU SEEN MY FATHER AND MOTHER AND SISTERS AND BROTHERS GO BY?"

But by the time Walter had said "seen" all the creatures stopped their singing and he found himself shouting, shouting loudly in the quiet night.

Walter was so embarrassed to find himself making such a noise, he did not know what to do. All around him he saw hundreds of faces looking silently at him. Now it was so still Walter was afraid to move.

At last the great huge creature came galumphing over to him and in a great deep voice he asked, "What did you say?"

Walter was so frightened he could hardly speak, but at last he managed to say, "Ha-have yo-you se-seen my father and mother and sisters and brothers go by?"

By now all the strange creatures had gathered around Walter. Instead of answering him, the Huge One turned to them and asked, "Have you seen his father and mother and sisters and brothers go by?"

Then they each asked each other, "Have you seen his father and mother and sisters and brothers go by?" Then they all sang together, "No-no-no, no, no."

Walter began to sob.

"What is the matter?" asked the Huge One.

"I am hungry, sir," sobbed Walter.

"Why don't you eat then?" said the Huge One.

"But I have nothing to eat, sir," said Walter.

"Well, look around and find something," said the Huge One.

So Walter looked around and he found some seeds to eat and he ate a great many, but then he felt so sleepy he began to cry again.

"What is the matter?" asked the Huge One.

"I am sleepy and I have no bed, sir."

"But if you are sleepy why don't you just sleep?" said the Huge One. "Shut your eyes and go to sleep."

"Go to sleep, shut your eyes and go to sleep, go to sleep, to sleep, to sleep," sang all the pond creatures together while the Huge One sang in his great deep voice, "To—sleep," "To—sleep," "Tooooo—sleeeeep."

HOW WALTER
FINDS A NEW HOME

Walter was very tired, but he did not sleep late the next morning because the pond creatures were awake and bustling about.

When he opened his eyes he saw that three very green creatures were sitting near him, staring at him with their great eyes and smiling with their wide mouths. He heard one whisper to another, "It's a mouse," and the other said, "Wonder where it came from?"

Now Walter was a polite mouse and although he was very sleepy he managed to say, "Good morning."

They all said, "Good morning," very cheerfully, but then they said nothing more as they sat there staring and smiling.

Walter tried to think of something more to say. At last he said, "My name is Walter Mouse. What is yours?"

"Frog," said the first creature. "Frog," said the second creature. "Frog," said the third creature.

"But what are your first names?" asked Walter.

"That's all," said the three frogs together.

"Dear me," said Walter, "how do you tell each other apart?"

"I always know who I am," said the first frog, and the second said, "I do too," and the third said, "So do I."

"But," said Walter, "how does anyone else know who is which?"

"It doesn't really matter," they all answered together.

"Oh," said Walter. "But wouldn't you like to have names just to be different?"

"It might be nice," said the first. "If they were nice names," said the second. "Do you know any nice names?" asked the third.

"Oh, lots and lots of them," said Walter, and he named some. "Peter, Mary, John, Nancy, Lulu."

"I like that one," said the first frog.

"But it makes a difference if you are a boy or a girl," said Walter.

"I don't care," said the first one.

So the first frog was named Lulu. And Walter went on, "There is George, Joan, Alice, Leander."

"I like that one," said the second frog.

So the second frog was named Leander. And Walter went on, "There is Edward, Henry, Peggy, Richard, Dorothy, Percy."

"I like that one," said the third frog, so the third frog was named Percy.

"Come swim with us?" said Lulu.

"But I left my bathing suit at home," said Walter.

When Walter said "home," he began to feel very sad again. And he said, "I don't know where my home is!" and tears rolled down his cheeks.

"Oh, dear, oh, dear," said Lulu as she saw Walter's tears. "Let's ask The Frog what to do."

"Who is The Frog?" asked Walter.

"Oh, he is The Frog and all others are just frogs," explained Leander.

So they led Walter over to a huge creature who lay near the water's edge. It was the same huge creature Walter had talked to the night before.

Lulu explained carefully that Walter was un-happy because he did not know where his home was. The Frog only blinked his eyes and said, "It doesn't really matter."

"But I need a home. I miss it, sir," said Walter.

"Why don't you find one here?" said The Frog.

"Oh, yes, do find one here!" said Lulu.

"But where shall I find it?" asked Walter.

"Now let me see," said The Frog, and he swung slowly around in the water, looking about with his great eyes. By the time he was halfway around he seemed to get tired and he settled down in the water with only his nose above, and his bulging eyes looked dreamy.

Just as Walter was wondering if it would be polite to remind him about where to find a home, The Frog came puffing up to the surface of the water again. "Find your home on the island," he said.

Walter looked out over the water and sure enough, almost hidden by the green leaves of the water plants, he saw a beautiful little island not far from the shore.

"Give it a name," said Leander.

Walter hesitated. "Will the whole island be all mine, sir?" he asked.

"Of course," said The Frog.

"Let me name it," begged Lulu. "I know an ele-gant name for it. Let's name it Mouse Island!"

"Yes, yes," sang all three frogs together, "and you will be The Mouse of Mouse Island!" And they all jumped into the pond with a great splash and Walter could see them swimming swiftly through the clear water toward Mouse Island.

But Walter did not move from the shore; there he stood looking very lonely.

"Why don't you swim out to your island?" asked The Frog.

"I have no bathing suit, sir!" said Walter.

"That's too bad," said The Frog, and he settled down to doze in the sun.

Soon Lulu and Leander and Percy all came swimming back for him.

"Hurry up and swim to Mouse Island," they called to Walter.

"But I can't," said Walter. "Don't you remember I told you I have no bathing suit?"

Lulu and Leander and Percy only looked rather blankly at Walter and said, "Did you?"

The Frog slowly crawled up beside Walter.

"Turtle might take you," he said.

"We will ask him," said all three frogs, and they disappeared in the water, but soon they were back again and with them came a large box turtle swimming through the water with just his head and his high shell above the surface. The Turtle came up to where Walter stood and crawled up on the shore. He smiled at Walter and said:

"Hop on, sir." Carefully Walter climbed upon his back and they were off to Mouse Island.

Lulu and Leander and Percy reached the island

first, but they waited among the lily pads for Walter and the Turtle.

Carefully, the Turtle climbed up on the shore and Walter slid down from his back and looked about him.

Overhead the water plants made a green bower and the soft velvet green moss grew over the ground.

"Welcome to your island, Sir Mouse," said the Turtle, bowing his head.

Walter was surprised to hear himself called "Sir Mouse."

"Thank you for the ride," he said politely, "but I don't think my name is 'Sir Mouse,' it has always been Walter Mouse before."

"Oh, but now you are The Mouse of Mouse Island!" said the Turtle, and he looked so polite and respectful Walter felt very important for the first time in his life.

Then the three frogs came bouncing up. "Welcome to your island, Sir Mouse!" they all said together, bowing very low.

This made Walter feel so important he was a little uncomfortable.

"I wish you would call me just 'Walter,'" he said.

"As you like," said Lulu; "but it is easier to call you Sir Mouse."

"Or if you like two names," suggested Percy, "we might call you 'Mouse Mouse.'"

"It doesn't matter," added Leander. So always after that they called Walter "Mouse Mouse" because it was easier to remember.

"Doesn't the Turtle have any name?" asked Walter, changing the subject.

"Oh, no," said Lulu, "he is just 'Turtle!'"

"Wouldn't you like a name?" Walter asked the Turtle. "I know lots of names."

But Turtle showed no interest in the matter, in fact, he rather rudely pulled his head into his shell along with his feet and his hands and his tail and Walter found himself talking to what looked like an empty shell.

"He does that," said Lulu. "He does that quite often."

"Oh," said Walter.

"This is a nice home," said Percy, looking about him.

"But there is no house!" said Walter.

"House?" asked Leander. "House?" asked Percy. "What do you mean by house?" asked Lulu.

"Why, you must have a house to have a home," said Walter, "a home is a house."

"What does a house look like, Mouse Mouse?" asked Lulu.

Walter tried to explain, "My house had an inside and an outside and a front door and a back door and stairs and a roof and a chimney and a kitchen and—"

"Do all houses have to ha
asked Percy.

"Oh, no," said Walter, "bu
have an inside and an outs
a doorway so you can go insid

"Then why don't you make
asked Lulu.

Now Walter was a lazy m
lonely without a home he got
himself a little house on his i
small twigs and of grasses and
an outside and a roof and the
he could go inside of it. By th
the sun had set and Walter w
he had never worked so hard
good night to the three frogs
went inside his house and la
which made a soft green carp
to sleep—sound asleep within
under his own roof.

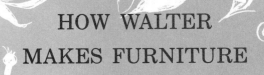

HOW WALTER
MAKES FURNITURE

When he woke up the next day Walter looked up at his own roof and at his own walls but he felt that something was missing. "Oh, dear me," said Walter, "I forgot the furniture!"

He went outdoors and to his surprise there he found Lulu and Leander and Percy already waiting for him.

"Good morning," he said. "It is nice of you to come to call so early."

"We didn't come," said Lulu.

"Why, you must have come," said Walter, "or you would not be here."

"Oh, no," said Lulu, "we did not come because we never went away."

"You see," explained Leander, "we live here now, we like it here."

"That's very nice," said Walter. "Would you like me to help build you a house to live in? I am afraid there is not enough room in my house for us all to sleep at night."

"Thank you," said Percy, "we don't need a house."

"But won't you miss a house for a home?" asked Walter.

"Oh, no," said Lulu, laughing. "How could we miss something we have never had?"

"Then I am going to make myself some furniture," said Walter. "And I don't want you to see it until it is all done because I want to surprise you."

So Lulu and Leander and Percy went off to play while Walter made himself some furniture.

Walter spent a long time making the furniture for his new home. He made himself a beautiful bed out of twigs with a mattress of pine needles and he made himself a beautiful chair of twigs and grasses and he made himself a table, but since he had no nails or hammer he carefully tied all the pieces together with grasses as best he could.

"It doesn't matter," added Leander. So always after that they called Walter "Mouse Mouse" because it was easier to remember.

"Doesn't the Turtle have any name?" asked Walter, changing the subject.

"Oh, no," said Lulu, "he is just 'Turtle!'"

"Wouldn't you like a name?" Walter asked the Turtle. "I know lots of names."

But Turtle showed no interest in the matter, in fact, he rather rudely pulled his head into his shell along with his feet and his hands and his tail and Walter found himself talking to what looked like an empty shell.

"He does that," said Lulu. "He does that quite often."

"Oh," said Walter.

"This is a nice home," said Percy, looking about him.

"But there is no house!" said Walter.

"House?" asked Leander. "House?" asked Percy. "What do you mean by house?" asked Lulu.

"Why, you must have a house to have a home," said Walter, "a home is a house."

"What does a house look like, Mouse Mouse?" asked Lulu.

Walter tried to explain, "My house had an inside and an outside and a front door and a back door and stairs and a roof and a chimney and a kitchen and—"

"Do all houses have to have all those things?" asked Percy.

"Oh, no," said Walter, "but every house must have an inside and an outside and a roof and a doorway so you can go inside of it."

"Then why don't you make yourself a little one?" asked Lulu.

Now Walter was a lazy mouse, but he felt so lonely without a home he got very busy and made himself a little house on his island. He made it of small twigs and of grasses and it had an inside and an outside and a roof and there was a doorway so he could go inside of it. By the time it was finished the sun had set and Walter was very tired because he had never worked so hard in his life, so he said good night to the three frogs and Turtle. Then he went inside his house and lay down on the moss which made a soft green carpet floor and he went to sleep—sound asleep within his own walls and under his own roof.

When he was finished he called Lulu and Leander and Percy to come look. Even Turtle came. Although he was much too large to fit into the little house, he put his head through the doorway and he could see very nicely.

"See my beautiful bed," said Walter, pointing to the bed he had made.

"What is it for?" asked Percy.

"To sleep in like this," said Walter, climbing up on the bed and lying down, but crash! down fell the headboard and down fell the footboard and down fell the whole bed with Walter under the pieces.

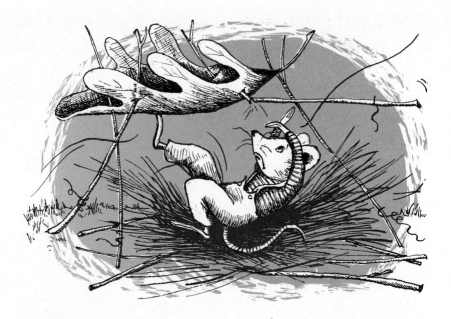

"Ha, ha, ha, ha," laughed the frogs together. "That's a funny way to sleep!"

Walter climbed out from under the pieces, and brushed the pine needles off his clothes; he looked very sad but then he went on as if nothing had happened. "Now," said he, "look at my beautiful chair." And he pointed to the beautiful chair which he had made.

"What's it for?" asked Leander.

"You sit in it like this," said Walter, and he sat down very carefully in the beautiful chair but crash! down he came on the floor and the chair came down in pieces on top of him!

"Ha, ha, ha, ha," laughed all the frogs together as Walter climbed out from under the pieces. "That is a funny way to sit down."

Walter did not say a word, he waited a moment and then he smiled and he pointed to the beautiful table he had made. "Look," he said, "look at the beautiful table I have made!"

"What's it for?" asked Lulu, all ready to begin to laugh again.

But Walter did not move, he just stood there and pointed at it. "That," said Walter, "is just made to look at."

"Oh," said Leander and Lulu and Percy all together, "but we liked the bed and chair better. Won't you make some more?"

"No," said Walter, shaking his head.

"No, I don't think really I need any furniture, except the table."

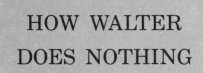

HOW WALTER
DOES NOTHING

The next day when Walter came out of his house there were Lulu and Leander and Percy waiting for him.

"Good morning, Mouse Mouse," they said. "What are you going to make for yourself today?"

"Good morning," said Walter. "I have my house and I have all the furniture I need so I am not going to make anything today."

"Then what are you going to do with yourself?" asked Lulu.

"Nothing," said Walter.

So Walter did nothing whatever all that day. The frogs were very busy swimming and jumping and singing together but Walter did nothing but eat, sleep, and be lazy.

Every morning for the next three days, he found Lulu, Leander, and Percy waiting for him when he came out of his house.

Each morning they would say, "Good morning, Mouse Mouse, and what are you doing today?"

And each morning Walter would say, "Nothing," and he did nothing—he did not play with them or talk with them for the rest of the day.

On the fourth day, when Walter came out of his house in the morning, Lulu, Leander, and Percy were not waiting to wish him "Good morning."

Walter could see them playing together out on the lily pads but they did not come near him.

Walter did nothing but be lazy as usual, but after a while he grew tired of being lazy. He grew tired of doing nothing because he was lonely.

So very carefully he stepped on one of the lily pads nearest the shore and he walked on tiptoes over it to the next one and then he hopped from one lily pad to another until he was quite far from shore and near where Leander and Lulu and Percy were swimming.

"Good morning," he called to them. "Good morning."

Lulu and Leander and Percy climbed up one at a time and sat on the lily pad near him. "Good morning," they said politely, but they looked at Walter strangely. They looked at him as if they had never seen him before.

He heard Lulu whisper to Leander, "It's a mouse. I wonder where he came from?"

He heard Leander whisper to Percy, "Say something. It isn't polite to stare at a stranger that way."

"I am not a stranger," said Walter. "I am Walter. I am Walter Mouse. I am your friend Mouse Mouse!"

But they only looked at him with their large eyes and smiled politely and Walter knew then that they had forgotten him completely.

"My name is Frog," said Lulu, and Leander said, "My name is Frog," and Percy said, "My name is Frog."

And then Walter knew they had not only forgotten him and forgotten his name but they had forgotten their own names he had given them!

"Come swim with us!" they all said together, smiling pleasantly.

"But I have no bathing suit. Don't you remember I told you I have no bathing suit?" Then Walter began to cry—he cried because he felt so lonely and so strange because his friends the frogs did not remember him.

Just then Turtle came swimming up and by this time Walter was so sad and felt so strange he felt it was no use to wish Turtle good morning. He did not feel like himself, but to his surprise Turtle spoke to him. He said, "Good morning, Mouse Mouse!"

"Turtle, Turtle," Walter cried, running over. "Oh, Turtle, Turtle, Lulu and Leander and Percy have all forgotten me," he cried. "What shall I do?"

"That's strange," said Turtle. "Don't they live on your island? Don't they see you every day? Don't they play with you? Don't they play with you all the time?"

"Yes, they live on my island," said Walter, "but I have done nothing for quite a few days so they have seen little of me."

"Then that's why they forgot," said Turtle. "They just can't seem to help forgetting things, and if you were not around to remind them of course they forgot you!"

So Walter taught Lulu and Leander and Percy their names all over again and he showed them his house and his table. And though they did not seem to remember either having heard their names or Walter's name before, or having seen his house or his table before, they thought everything very nice and they were happy to be friends of Walter's all over again.

HOW WALTER
LEARNS TO SWIM

Walter never dared to be lazy again. He still remembered how his own family had moved away and forgotten him because he had been lazy, and, now that he knew his friends the frogs could not remember very long, he was very careful to be with them every moment of the day so they would not forget him again.

When he did take time out for a nap Walter would curl up inside a water lily to be near them while they sunned themselves on the lily pads. He tried to play the way they did. He learned to play leapfrog, and although his legs were much too short he managed to bounce over their backs very nicely. He even tried to learn to sing but without much success.

But always when they would ask him to come swim with them Walter would say, "No, I have no bathing suit." Still they never seemed to remember this and they would always ask him again and again, until one day Walter said, "I wish I could

swim with you but I have no bathing suit." Then
he thought awhile and said, "I could go swimming
in my underwear but I don't know how to swim
very well. I wish I could swim like you."

"We will teach you, we will teach you," said all
three frogs together.

So Walter took off his shoes and his socks and
his overalls and his blouse. Then he walked out to
the edge of a lily pad and he looked down; he
looked down into the clear deep water of the pond.

"Jump, jump, jump! and dive in!" sang the frogs.

Walter got ready to jump; he crouched low and
he rose on his toes all ready to spring into the air—
but he could not make himself jump.

He could not jump because he was afraid.

"I don't think I want to jump and dive in," he said, and he sat down on the edge of the lily pad. "I guess I'd rather just paddle my feet in the water instead."

So he sat there and paddled his feet in the water instead. Walter paddled his feet for quite a long time but all the time he was paddling he wanted to swim, he wanted to swim beautifully through the water as the frogs did. At last he said, "Maybe Turtle would help me."

"Help you what?" asked Lulu, who was resting in the water near by.

"Help me swim beautifully," said Walter.

"But Turtle isn't such a fine swimmer himself," said Lulu.

"But he can stay on top the water," said Walter, "and he might let me hold onto him."

"I will find him and ask him," said Lulu, and she swam off to find Turtle.

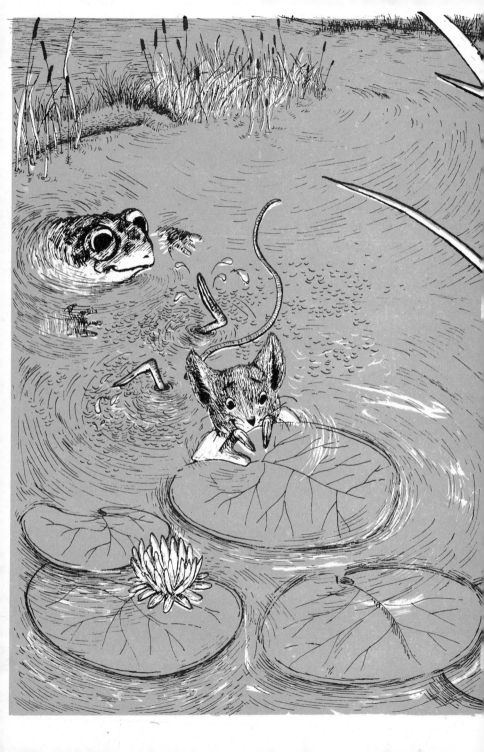

Soon she was back again with Turtle swimming along after her. Turtle was pleased to help Walter swim beautifully like the frogs.

"I will stay right here," he said as he paddled himself a little away from the lily pad where Walter was sitting.

So once again Walter stood up on the edge of the lily pad and got ready to jump.

"Jump, jump, jump! and dive in!" sang the frogs.

Walter shut his eyes tight and he jumped. He rose in the air and then down he came splash into the water. He felt the water all around him and he went down, down, down, and then he felt himself coming up, up, up, and then he opened his eyes and there was Turtle.

"Grab hold of my tail," shouted Turtle. "Grab hold!"

Quickly Walter grabbed hold of Turtle's tail with both his hands.

"Swim, swim, SWIM!" sang the frogs. "Kick out your legs and swim!"

"Kick out your legs like this," and they swam near Walter, kicking out their beautiful strong legs while they swam.

Slowly Turtle paddled through the water towing Walter behind him. Walter kicked his little legs, he kicked them faster and faster.

"Pull them up and kick them out!" sang the frogs. "Pull them up and kick them out."

But Walter's legs were too short. Try as he might he could not make them kick out like the frogs.

Walter turned to look at his legs kicking, but as he turned his hands slipped from Turtle's tail and Walter felt himself going down.

"Push with your hands, push with your hands!" sang the frogs.

So Walter pushed with his hands and he kicked with his legs while the frogs kept singing, "Swim, swim, kick and swim, push with your hands and kick with your legs, pull them up and kick them out, push, kick, push, kick, swim, swim, SWIM!"

Then they shouted, "Stop paddling—do it this way—this way." Then they said, "Ha-ha-ha. Your legs aren't much of a much for swimming." For poor Walter could only paddle and puff, paddle and puff slowly through the water.

At last he reached a lily pad near the shore. Slowly he climbed upon it for he felt very tired and wet and sad because he could not swim beautifully like the frogs. He was so wet his fur stuck closely to him and his whiskers hung limply down. The frogs climbed up beside him. Walter began to shiver and shake with the cold and then he began to sneeze, "Ketch-choo, ketch-choo!"

Now the frogs did not know what it meant to be cold. Their satin-smooth skins were shiny and fresh whether wet or dry. They thought Walter was playing a game.

"Catch you, catch you!" they cried, and started to chase Walter, jumping over the lily pads. Walter ran lightly away from them. "Run, run, run," he shouted as he saw them jumping awkwardly, and they tried, but they were clumsy and fell all in a heap.

"Oh, oh, oh!" laughed Walter. "Your legs aren't much of a much for running!" The frogs began to laugh, too, and soon Walter and Lulu and Leander and Percy were laughing so hard they quite forgot what they were laughing about and Walter was warm and dry again.

HOW WALTER
TEACHES SCHOOL

As the days and nights went by, Walter quite forgot about time. He was so busy doing things with his friends, the frogs, all the time so they would not forget him that he was no longer a slow and lazy young mouse.

One day he began to wonder how many days he had lived on Mouse Island. He asked the frogs if they knew but they did not seem to know what he meant.

"Don't you know how to count?" he asked, but they did not know what counting meant.

"Don't you know how to write?" he asked, but they did not know what writing meant.

"Don't you know how to read?" Walter asked, but the frogs did not know what reading meant.

"Have you never been to school?" he asked.

"School?" asked the frogs. "What is school?"

"I will show you," said Walter.

"First you must sit all in a row and I will be the

teacher and you will be my pupils. But we should have desks and seats."

"Make some," said Percy.

Now Walter was not sure just how good he was about making furniture since the bed and chair had crashed. He looked around him and then he said, "I know what we can use," and then he found some nice toadstools growing near by, big ones and little ones, and he used the big ones for desks and the little ones for seats.

"And you can write on the desks," said Walter, "as if they were slates."

Just then Turtle came by.

"Turtle, Turtle," called Lulu, "come here, we are going to play school!"

So Turtle joined them. "What kind of a game is

that?" he asked, and Walter said, "It isn't a game, it is real. This is a real school."

Then he showed Lulu and Leander and Percy how to sit nicely on their toadstool seats with their hands folded in front of them, but when he came to Turtle it was not so easy. Turtle was so large and awkward he would not fit on his seat so Walter finally arranged him by having him sit on the ground.

First Walter taught his pupils to sing the good-morning song. He taught them to sing:

"Good morning to you,
Good morning to you,
Good morning, dear teacher,
Good morning to you."

Then Walter called the roll, but Lulu had forgotten her name again.

"This will never do, Lulu," said Walter. "You must write your name ten times after school."

Now Lulu, of course, did not know how to write at all so she did not know Walter meant to punish her, so she said, "Thank you."

"Now we will learn to count," said Walter quickly. "Say one, Lulu." So Lulu said, "One."

Then Walter asked Leander and Percy to say two and three, but when he came to Turtle, he was inside his shell fast asleep.

"Wake up! Wake up!" shouted Walter, tapping on Turtle's shell. Out came Turtle's head. "Say four," said Walter. "Four!" shouted Turtle and went to sleep again. Over and over, Walter asked them to count, but Turtle either would say "Four" at the wrong time or stay asleep.

Then Walter taught them to add and subtract. He taught them that two and two make five and that five from eleven leaves seven, because Walter had been such a lazy pupil in school himself that he did not know he was wrong. He taught them that k-a-t spells cat and r-i-t-e spells "write," and since neither the frogs nor Turtle nor Walter knew any better it did not make much difference and Walter felt very important to be a schoolteacher.

"Now remember to be on time tomorrow," Walter said as he dismissed the class.

'hat's why they forget," whispered Turtle to
er.

Walter did not try to explain any more. It
already getting late and the sun was beginning
t.

ook," he said, pointing to the sun. "Turtle,
bring them to school when the sun rises in the
ing."

, every morning when the sun rose in the sky,
er was very careful to be at school early to
ome his pupils and he never dared be even a
lazy because he was teaching the frogs to be
ime.

"What is time?" asked Lulu who had never had any reason to know about time before.

"Time is something you tell by the clock," said Walter.

"But we have no clock," said Percy.

"So we can't be on it," said Leander.

"So it doesn't matter," they all said together.

"Oh, yes, it matters," said Walter. "Time always matters."

"Then what is time?" asked Lulu all over again, and Walter tried to explain all over again although he had never thought much about it himself before.

"It's this way," he said, "time is when today turns into yesterday and tomorrow turns into today."

"What is yesterday?" asked Lulu.

"What is today?" asked Leander.

"What is tomorrow?" asked Percy.

"That's why they forget," whispered Turtle to Walter.

So Walter did not try to explain any more. It was already getting late and the sun was beginning to set.

"Look," he said, pointing to the sun. "Turtle, you bring them to school when the sun rises in the morning."

So, every morning when the sun rose in the sky, Walter was very careful to be at school early to welcome his pupils and he never dared be even a little lazy because he was teaching the frogs to be on time.

HOW WALTER
NEEDS HIS COAT

The days passed so quickly that summer was soon over and Walter began to feel chilly in the cool mornings of the fall.

The legs of his overalls and the sleeves of his blouse were much too short, for Walter had grown longer since he had first come to Mouse Island. His legs were longer, his arms were longer, his ears were longer. His tail was longer and even his whiskers were longer. Also, Walter needed a coat, but he had no coat, because he had worn neither coat nor hat that day in the spring when he had started out to find his family.

"I wish I had a coat," he said one day to Lulu and Leander and Percy and Turtle, "I am cold!" And he shivered.

"What is cold?" asked Lulu.

"When you are warm you are not cold," said Walter, "and when you are cold you are not warm. If I had a coat I would be warm but I haven't any coat so I am cold!" And he shivered again.

"What is a coat?" asked Lulu.

"It is a jacket to keep you warm," said Walter. "I need more clothes on!"

"You have more clothes on than I have," said Lulu. "I haven't any clothes at all, oh-hhheoo. I am cold, too." And she shivered just as Walter had done.

"You're silly," said Leander to Lulu. "You're silly. How can you be cold without any clothes when you have never had any?"

But Lulu still shivered.

"You silly," said Percy, "I suppose you will begin to need a house next!"

"No, I don't care about a house," said Lulu. "But I would like some clothes just like Mouse Mouse."

"Girls don't have clothes like mine," Walter said. "Girls wear skirts."

"I want a skirt, I want a skirt," cried Lulu.

Now this was the first time Walter had heard Lulu or Leander or Percy wish for something they did not have.

"Poor Lulu," he said. "Poor Lulu, what shall we do?"

"Make one," suggested Leander.

"Make a skirt," said Percy.

So Walter made a skirt for Lulu. He made it of small fern leaves and he tied them carefully around Lulu's waist with a blade of grass for a sash. And it was a beautiful skirt because it had a long, sweeping train like a queen's.

Lulu felt strange to have a skirt on; and at first she was afraid to move. Then she discovered she could swish it. She swished it this way and that way while Walter and Leander and Percy and Turtle all admired it.

"Let's show The Frog," said Walter, who was very proud of the skirt he had made. "Let's show The Frog and all the other frogs in the pond."

"Yes, yes!" exclaimed Lulu, jumping for joy, but

alas, as Lulu jumped, off came her sash, off came her skirt, and there lay the fern leaves scattered on the ground!

"Ha, ha, ha," laughed Leander and Percy and Turtle. "Ha, ha!"

But Walter did not laugh. "Oh, look what you have done, Lulu!" he cried. "Look what you have done. You should not jump when you have a skirt on!"

"But I have to jump," sobbed Lulu; "but I have to jump!"

"Make another, make another, make another," said Leander and Percy and Turtle.

But Walter only shook his head sadly. "It's no use," he said. "It's no use, it will always fall off when she jumps."

"Your clothes don't fall off when you jump," Lulu said.

"But they are made of cloth," said Walter, and then he began to think of his own clothes again and this made him shiver again. "I'm cold," he said. "I'm cold without any coat on."

"And I'm cold," complained Lulu. "I'm cold without any skirt on!"

They both looked so miserable and shivered so hard that Leander and Percy began to shiver, too.

"I'm cold," said Leander.

"I'm cold," said Percy.

Only Turtle said nothing; he tucked himself into his shell, disappearing completely, but soon he came out again. "Why don't you go to Mouse Village and get some clothes?" he said.

"But I don't know where Mouse Village is," said Walter. "I lost it and I lost my family and I am lost, lost, lost, and I need my coat," and he cried because he was lost and he was cold.

"But I know," said Turtle.

"Know what?" asked Walter.

"Know where Mouse Village is," said Turtle calmly. "I go by that way quite often."

Walter was so surprised that he stopped crying. "Why didn't you tell me before?" he asked.

"You never asked me," said Turtle.

"Take me back," cried Walter, "take me back to Mouse Village!"

"Now?" asked Turtle.

"Will you bring back a skirt for me, Mouse Mouse?" asked Lulu, and Leander and Percy begged him to bring back clothes for them, too, because now they wanted them more than ever.

"I don't know where to get any, I don't know where my family went to," said Walter, remembering again. "But last year Miss Gray, my teacher, collected clothes for the needy."

"We need clothes, we need clothes, we need clothes," sang Lulu and Leander and Percy dolefully, and Walter felt very sorry for them.

"Come, Turtle," he said, "take me to Mouse Village and I will ask Miss Gray for clothes for the needy."

So Walter climbed upon Turtle's back and away they went, across the pond to the mainland on their way to Mouse Village.

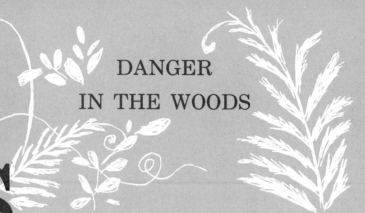

DANGER
IN THE WOODS

Slowly Turtle made his way under tall ferns and over gnarled roots of towering trees and Walter clung to his slippery back tightly with both knees. Soon the last rays of the sun disappeared and they traveled along in the increasing darkness of the night.

Walter grew sleepy as they lurched along, so sleepy that his head began to nod, and he swayed this way and that way, and before he knew what had happened he forgot to hold on and down he slid, off Turtle's slippery back.

But Turtle went on as if nothing had happened because he did not know that Walter was no longer with him.

"Turtle, Turtle, wait for me!" cried Walter as he picked himself up. But Turtle did not hear him as he shoved on through the darkness of the night.

Walter could hear Turtle scrambling through the underbrush but he could not see him. He stumbled over the ground following the noise.

"Turtle, Turtle, wait for me!" he called, but still
Turtle did not hear him so he did not stop.

At last Walter caught up to Turtle. He tried to
climb up onto Turtle's moving back. He was almost
up when Turtle gave a sudden lurch and down fell
Walter again, but this time, as he fell, he grabbed
Turtle's tail with both hands.

Turtle stopped instantly and cried, "Danger, hide,
hide yourself quick!" and he drew himself quickly
into his shell, shutting it tight. Walter scuttled to a
rock close by and there he hid himself in a crack.
He crouched there and peered into the darkness

and listened. He could see nothing and he could hear nothing but the wind moaning.

Could it be an owl hovering overhead? Could it be a snake, a snake creeping, slipping through the grass? Walter did not know. He did not know what it could be, so he crouched there in the crack in the rock and waited. He dared not call to Turtle, he dared not leave the rock, so there he stayed waiting, waiting for he knew not what. Walter stayed there all through the night until the first gray light of dawn showed through the trees and then he saw Turtle's head come peering out from his shell and looking carefully around him. The Turtle called to Walter, "It's all right, it is safe to go on."

So Walter came running over to him. He was stiff from being still so long but he quickly climbed up again and they were off.

"What was it? What was the danger?" Walter asked Turtle as they jogged along.

"I don't know," said Turtle, "but something grabbed my tail from behind. Did you see anything?" ·

"No, I didn't see anything," said Walter, and then he remembered. "Oh, Turtle, Turtle," he cried, "it was not danger, it was only me!"

"You should say 'It was only I,'" said Turtle rather severely.

They were hurrying along very fast now. Soon they were on a road and Walter saw the roofs and the church steeple of Mouse Village not far away.

WALTER RETURNS HOME

Walter was so excited when he saw Mouse Village so near that he slid off Turtle's back and this time he did not climb up again. He scampered along beside Turtle. "Here we come to the baseball field," he cried. "This is where I used to play baseball!"

"I will leave you here," said Turtle, "and I will come back for you at sundown."

"But won't you come with me?" asked Walter. "I'd like to show you my school and Main Street and—"

"No thank you," said Turtle. "I must be on my way."

"Where to?" asked Walter.

"Oh, here and there," said Turtle, and he left Walter there at the ball field just outside Mouse Village.

The morning was yet very early and the sun was still rosy from its rising. Walter felt strange to be up and about in Mouse Village at such an early

hour. It looked different from the way he remembered it. He knew it was too early to go to school, but since he did not know where else to go he went to the schoolhouse and sat on the steps. As he sat there, Walter began to wonder if perhaps it were September yet. If it were August, there would be no school and then he did not know what he would do. "Oh, dear," said Walter to himself. "Oh, dear, what shall I do and where shall I go?"

But then, just then, at that moment he saw Miss Gray coming up the road with some books under her arm.

"Oh, Miss Gray!" Walter called, running to meet her. "Good morning, Miss Gray!"

Miss Gray was so surprised to see Walter she dropped her books.

"My goodness sakes!" she exclaimed. "My goodness sakes! Walter Mouse, how you did startle me! I have never seen you at school so early in the morning! You are always so late. I have hardly noticed you at all lately!"

"But I haven't been in school lately," said Walter. "I haven't been here at all because I was somewhere else!"

"That's the trouble," said Miss Gray. "You just don't pay attention to what is going on about you."

Now Walter was so upset because Miss Gray had not even missed him he did not know just quite how to ask her about clothes for the frogs. Before he could bring himself to mention it, she said, "Since you are such a good little mouse today, Walter, you may ring the bell to call the others to school."

So Walter stood on the school steps and he rang the bell calling the others to school. Soon they began coming, coming up the road, and the first to arrive were Walter's five brothers and six sisters.

When they saw Walter ringing the school bell they came running up to him and all the time that he was ringing the bell they were shouting at him with joy.

"Walter, Walter, where did you come from?" they asked.

"I have been away," shouted Walter as he kept on ringing the bell, and he shouted still louder so they could hear him above the dingdong of the bell. "Did you miss me?"

"Yes, we missed you," they shouted back. "We missed you because there was one too many beds," said one of his sisters. "And one too many chairs," said one of his brothers. "But it is all right now," shouted another brother. "It is all right now because—"

But before he could finish Miss Gray called, "Time for roll call."

So Walter and all his brothers and sisters and all the other children went into the schoolhouse and sat down at their desks.

Walter sat in his old seat at his old desk but he was not the same Walter who had sat there in the spring because he was no longer lazy. He watched and listened very carefully to all that Miss Gray did and said because he wanted to learn new things to teach the frogs.

Walter heard Miss Gray ask one of his sisters, "How much are two and two?"

And he heard his sister say, "Four."

"Correct!" said Miss Gray to Walter's great surprise.

Walter heard Miss Gray ask a little mouse boy, "If you take seven from eleven, how much have you left?"

"Four," said the little mouse boy.

"Correct," said Miss Gray, and Walter was surprised.

And he heard that "write" is not spelled r-i-t-e, and soon Walter discovered he had taught the frogs all wrong!

So he decided then and there that he would not go back to the frogs right away. He might better stay in Mouse Village and come to school every day and learn all he could so that he would be able to teach the frogs correctly.

At lunch-time Walter's brothers and sisters came running over to him and said, "Come hurry home with us and surprise Mother!"

So Walter hurried home with them and he hid behind them while they said to their mother, "Guess what we found?"

Walter's mother could not guess so she gave up, and out jumped Walter!

"My goodness gracious," she cried, "if it isn't Walter!" And she looked at him in his too small clothes and said, "How you have grown!"

"And I need my coat," he said.

"My goodness gracious, your coat would be too small now," his mother said. Then she gave Walter a whole new set of clothes with a coat and everything which his next older brother had outgrown.

So Walter felt very happy because he was back home and his family all remembered him and he had clothes which fitted him with a coat and everything. He told them all about Lulu and Leander and Percy and Turtle and how he had taught them to read and to write and to do arithmetic, and how much they needed clothes and how he must meet Turtle at the ball field and give him the clothes to take back. "I would like to live at home now," he added, "so I can go to school, and because I don't want you to forget me again."

"Dear me," said his mother, "that will be very nice but we will have to do something about a bed.

"But you have my bed, haven't you?" asked Walter.

"Oh, yes, we have what used to be your bed," she said. "But we have a surprise to show you!"

So they all went upstairs and there on Walter's bed were sleeping two new baby mice brothers and one new sister. "They came while you were away," said his mother, "so it was handy to have the extra bed. But," she added, "we will get them a bed of their own and you can have your own bed all to yourself. Now hurry off to school and I will have some clothes all ready for you to take to your friend the Turtle to take to the frogs."

So Walter hurried back to school. After school he went home.

His mother had ready a beautiful dress for Lulu and a pair of overalls for Leander and a sailor suit for Percy, and to his surprise his mother had embroidered their names on each one. "They will like that," she said, "because you have taught them to read."

Walter tied the clothes into a neat bundle and his mother gave him some string to fasten it to Turtle's back and Walter went out to the baseball field.

There was Turtle waiting for him. He was there, but he was hiding inside his shell. "Turtle, Turtle, come out," shouted Walter, knocking on the shell.

Out came Turtle's head and then out came his hands and his feet and tail. He rose and stretched himself and said, "Hop on, Mouse Mouse, we must hurry back or the frogs might forget you."

"But I am not going, Turtle," said Walter, and he explained to Turtle all about how he had decided to stay and how he must go to school because he had taught Turtle and the frogs all wrong.

"That doesn't matter," said Turtle. "That doesn't matter, because they will forget what you have taught them."

But Walter still felt that he should teach them correctly, so he tied the bundle tightly on Turtle's back and he said, "Come for me when the first hot day of summer comes and I will meet you at sunset here."

So Walter said good-by to Turtle and Turtle went back to Mouse Island and Walter went back to Mouse Village to be with his family and to go to school.

WALTER GOES BACK
TO MOUSE ISLAND

All winter long Walter was a busy young mouse. He was the very first of all his large family to be up in the morning. He was through with his breakfast first and on his way to school first. And every morning he would be the very first pupil in school, because Walter had become so used to being up and at school at sunrise on Mouse Island he no longer knew how to be lazy.

Every morning Miss Gray would let him ring the bell to call the others to school. And, all day long, Walter would pay attention to his lessons and he would give his answers promptly and correctly. Walter was such a very good pupil Miss Gray would often say, "What ever should we do without Walter!"

When the first hot day of summer vacation began, Walter said good-by to his mother and his father and his seven sisters and his seven brothers and they all said, "We will miss you."

Then Walter met Turtle as they had planned and he climbed upon Turtle's back and they set out to go back to Mouse Island.

"Did Lulu and Leander and Percy like the clothes?" Walter asked as they jogged along.

"Oh, yes, they were delighted with them," said Turtle. "But they always forget."

"Forget what?" asked Walter.

"Which clothes are whose," said Turtle.

"But they had their names on them," said Walter.

"Yes, but they always forget," said Turtle. "They forget whose names are which!"

Then Walter asked, "What about me? Have they forgotten me?"

"Of course," said Turtle.

"Well," said Walter, "I will have to teach them all over again."

By the time Walter and Turtle reached Mouse Island, it was the middle of the night. Lulu and Leander and Percy were nowhere in sight and Walter was very disappointed. "I thought they would come to meet me," he said.

"It is because they have forgotten," said Turtle.

"Yes, of course," said Walter.

"You had better get some sleep and I will bring them to school at sunrise in the morning," said Turtle. So Walter went to sleep in the little house he had made for himself so long ago, and when the sun rose in the morning he was up and out waiting for Lulu and Leander and Percy to come to school.

At last he saw them coming with Turtle leading the way, but they did not come swimming through the water beautifully as they used to do. No, they came hopping clumsily over the lily pads and then Walter saw the reason why.

Lulu and Leander and Percy were all dressed up in the clothes he had sent them, but such a sight they were! Leander had Lulu's dress on and Lulu had Percy's suit on wrong side to. Percy wore Leander's overalls without fastening the straps so he had to hold on to them all the time to keep them from falling off.

"It is time I came to teach them," said Walter to himself.

"Good morning," Walter called to them. "Good morning."

But Lulu and Leander and Percy behaved in the same way as they had when he first met them.

They looked at him with their large eyes smiling politely but said nothing. Then Walter heard Lulu whisper to Leander, "It's a mouse," and he heard Leander whisper to Percy, "Wonder where it came from?"

"I am Walter Mouse, your friend Mouse Mouse," said Walter patiently.

"My name is Frog," said Lulu and Leander and Percy all at the same moment, and Walter knew they had forgotten him and his name and their own names again, but this time he was not surprised

to know this, so he did not feel sad. It did not take him long to teach them their names and straighten out their clothes. So in no time at all they were all friends together again, and Walter was happy to be back on Mouse Island.

Every morning at sunrise, Walter would teach school, and he knew now that he was teaching Lulu and Leander and Percy correctly.

One morning, as he was teaching them how to count by tens Walter heard someone calling from

the mainland. He heard someone calling, "Walter, Walter!"

He looked across to the shore and there he saw his father and his mother and his seven sisters and his seven brothers.

Walter could hardly believe his eyes. "It is my family," he cried. "It is my family come to see me!"

"How do we get over to Mouse Island?" shouted his father.

"I'll send Turtle," Walter shouted back.

So Walter sent Turtle to ferry them over by twos and by threes, and soon Walter's whole family were on Mouse Island.

"We have come to spend the day," said his mother. "We missed you so much we just had to see how you were getting along."

"You ought to do something about the roads," said Walter's father. "Such a time we had to get here!"

Walter was very proud to have his family meet
Lulu and Leander and Percy. He was very proud of
his friends the frogs in their beautiful new clothes
and he had them show off how they could read and
write and do arithmetic correctly. Then he showed
his family his little house and his beautiful table.

"We can eat our lunch off your table," said one
of his brothers.

"No," said Walter. "That table is just made to
look at."

So they all had a merry picnic out of doors. Then the triplets took a nap inside a pond lily for a bed while the other young mice all took turns riding on Turtle's back.

When the triplets woke up Turtle took care of them while Walter and all the rest of Walter's large family and Lulu and Leander and Percy all played leapfrog together until the sun went down.

When it came time to go home they all said "Good-by" and thanked Walter for a very pleasant day. And Walter said he would come back to them in the winter and Walter's father said, "I am very proud of you, my son!"

And Walter's mother said, "Now don't forget us!"

Walter waved and waved as his family left for home and he was a very proud and important young mouse indeed. "GOOD-BY!"